HarperCollins TREASURY of Picture Book Classics

HarperCollins
TREASURY
of
Picture
Book
Classics

A Child's First Collection

HarperCollinsPublishers

HarperCollins Treasury of Picture Book Classics
A Child's First Collection
Introduction copyright © 2002 by Valerie Lewis
Page 439–440 serves as an extension of the copyright page.
Manufactured in China. All rights reserved.
www.harperchildrens.com

Library of Congress Cataloging-in-Publication Data
HarperCollins treasury of picture book classics : a child's
first collection / Margaret Wise Brown . . . [et al.].
      p.   cm.
  Summary: Contains twelve full-sized reproductions of
classic picture books accompanied by background
information for the reader.
  ISBN 0-06-008094-9
  1. Children's stories.   [1. Short stories.]
PZ5.H25 2002   2002002155
[E]—dc21   CIP
                                             AC

Typography by Alyssa Morris
1 2 3 4 5 6 7 8 9 10
❖
First Edition

"Most children . . . will react creatively
to the best work of a truly creative person."

—URSULA NORDSTROM,
in a letter to Mary V. Gaver
November 21, 1963

Contents

Introduction

With the birth of my first child, a devoted children's book enthusiast gave me *Goodnight Moon* by Margaret Wise Brown. It seemed so simple, which was not what I expected.

In the great green room
There was a telephone
And a red balloon
And a picture of—

As I read it to my toddler, I watched her eagerly anticipate each picture—a kitten, a mouse, the old lady whispering "hush." How many thousands of adults have read this aloud and had it repeated back to them by their children, who, when they have children, do the same? The power and awe in Brown's words and images have delighted families since the pages of *Goodnight Moon* were first turned in 1947.

The *HarperCollins Treasury of Picture Book Classics: A Child's First Collection* is a find for those who love children's books—an anthology that features twelve stunning classics, including Brown's masterpiece. These are the titles lauded without hesitation by parents, grandparents, librarians, teachers, and booksellers . . . a perfect collection to add to a child's home library.

Do we ever outgrow pictures? Picture books—drawings that tweak the imagination, ignite cognitive skills, and clarify the words that accompany them—when do we tire of them? Picture books introduce the art world, the aesthetics of color and form, the magic of images—critters, monsters, people, nature, and activity—that keep stories alive for generations.

Two highly coveted awards in the field of children's books—the Newbery Medal and the Caldecott Medal—are named after early advocates of picture books. In 1774, English publisher John Newbery illustrated what he called "instruction with delight" by putting small engravings of children at play in front of each "moral lesson" in his collection of nursery rhymes. Readers loved it. A teaching strategy was catching on: looking at a picture could reinforce a lesson as well as bring joy to the learner. When British artist Randolph Caldecott came along over a century later (1880), he enchanted readers with a kind of precursor to the comic book. In his illustrations of traditional nursery rhymes, Caldecott's dramatic, humorous images dominated the text, telling the story with pictures that progressed in a sequence. Now children would get used to reading images from left to right, just as they had learned to read letters.

Picture books help us to get to know our children. We see them react to various images, conflicts, and persons. We see them gravitate to one situation more than another. In turn, our responses teach them how *we* think and how we might react to a real dilemma. In this treasury, we meet Pete, whose father helps him out of a bad mood by turning the boy into a make-believe pizza; we sympathize with William, who, at odds with the precepts of maleness, really wants a doll; and we come to know the frustrations of Leo, a late bloomer. We discover a heroic boa constrictor named Crictor, who finds his home in France. We catch glimpses of two imaginative loners in George, who finds his adventures by shrinking, and Harold, who creates his world by drawing with a crayon. For those who face the arrival of a new sibling, Russell Hoban introduces us to Frances and her baby sister, and John Steptoe shows us how a twinkly-eyed infant and his older brother can get along.

Young children thrive on repetition and ask for the same story again and again. Certainly, a three-year-old's tolerance for hearing the same words repeatedly far surpasses mine. But there are books that give a child the delight of repetition while also offering a variety of rhythms, sounds, and moods. In those "Again!" moments, I turn to *Caps for Sale, If You Give a Mouse a Cookie,* and *From Head to Toe.*

It's clear that reading aloud regularly to a child is the best known way to build his or her vocabulary and to help make the child a reader. What do we know about pictures? We know that picture books with few words are the ones young children will memorize or repeat as stories in their own words. We know picture books can provide a visual experience that heightens the text, drawing young readers onward into the story. We know that picture books can reassure, improve listening, let us be downright silly, accelerate brain power, stretch the imagination, and offer a good excuse to be cozy. As a bonus to the pleasure of reading time together, we can share in the natural budding of a child's *appreciation of art* along with the building of his or her vocabulary.

Choosing books for children is not easy. From the thousands published each year, how can we pick the favorites that children will get to know by heart? I believe this treasury is a surefire place to start. It gives us diversity in the art, text, and subject matter. We can offer a child a wide range of experiences in listening and looking. Once your child has picked a favorite from this collection, he or she can find that story by itself in a picture book from a library or bookstore. Then, your child will have chosen which book to carry or to keep by his or her pillow for safekeeping. When your child is ready to move on to other titles, the library is waiting. It's such a pleasure to check out stacks of books from a library—our children's choices and ours—as we both experiment. Besides, encouraging the child to select is a way to help children build confidence in their ability to choose and to add gems to their own bookshelves.

Here's an ideal way to start: Dog-ear the pages of the dozen popular, time-tested stories here in this treasury. These are the children's choices, the classics and soon-to-be-classics, complete in both text and illustration. They have survived years of reading aloud and are here for the joy of the child in your life, and for you. We know that, even as adults, a particular image can bring back a memory of a picture book we've loved. What pleases me is that any gem from the collection can awaken memories. The delights in this treasury stay with you. When I hear a youngster call out at bedtime, "Goodnight Mommy, goodnight Daddy," I still find myself silently adding, "And goodnight to the old lady whispering 'hush.'" I have a feeling you'll find your own delight in each of these twelve classic stories.

—*Valerie Lewis*

HarperCollins

TREASURY

of

Picture

Book

Classics